Bears ODD Bears EVEN

A Puffin Math Easy-to-Read

by Harriet Ziefert
illustrated by Andrea Baruffi

PUFFIN BOOKS

PUFFIN BOOKS
Published by the Penguin Group
Penguin Books USA Inc., 375 Hudson Street, New York, New York 10014, U.S.A.
Penguin Books Ltd, 27 Wrights Lane, London W8 5TZ, England
Penguin Books Australia Ltd, Ringwood, Victoria, Australia
Penguin Books Canada Ltd, 10 Alcorn Avenue, Toronto, Ontario, Canada M4V 3B2
Penguin Books (N.Z.) Ltd, 182-90 Wairau Road, Auckland 10, New Zealand

Penguin Books Ltd, Registered Offices: Harmondsworth, Middlesex, England

First published by Viking, a division of Penguin Books USA Inc., 1997
Simultaneously published in Puffin Books

5 7 9 10 8 6 4

Text copyright © Harriet Ziefert, 1997
Illustrations copyright © Andrea Baruffi, 1997
All rights reserved

Library of Congress Catalog Card Number: 96-61640
ISBN 0-14-038539-8

Puffin® and Easy-to-Read® are registered trademarks of Penguin Books USA Inc.

Printed in U.S.A.
Set in New Century Schoolbook

Reading Level 1.8

Bears ODD Bears EVEN

Two, four, six, eight, ten—
even numbers.

Four polar bears playing—
an even number.

One, three, five, seven, nine—
odd numbers.

Five brown bears painting—
an odd number.

A brown bear in a tree
sees bears on a wall.
Some are big,
and some are small.

Count the bears.
Count the balls.
Which number is odd?
Which is even?

Six bears play tug-of-war—
three against three.

Which bears will win?
Wait and see.

Six bears play tug-of-war—
white against brown,

until three are up . . .
and three are down!

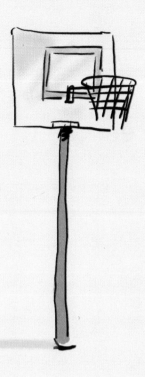

Five bears on a
basketball team.
That's odd.

Ten bears on two
basketball teams.

That's even.

4 cheerleaders for the yellow team.

2–4–6–8, who do we appreciate?

Yellow team, yellow team, yeah yellow!

3 cheerleaders for the red team.

3–5–7–9, who do we think is mighty fine?

Red team, red team, yeah red!

Three bears at school
learning some rules:
Even plus even—always even!

Odd plus odd—always even!

Odd plus even—always odd!

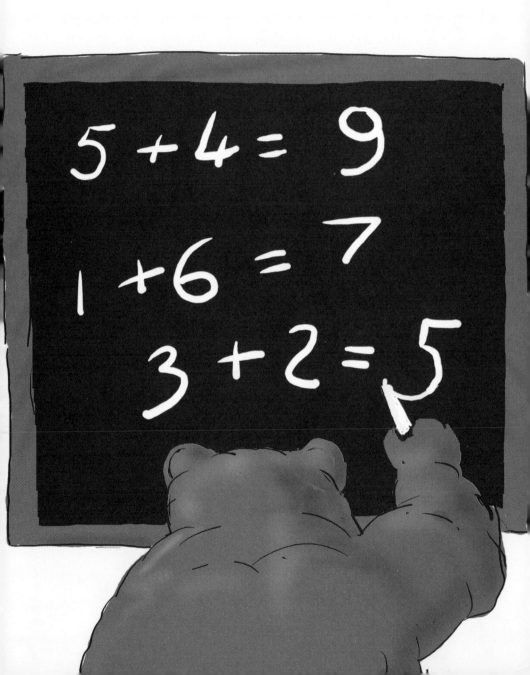

Five bears in a bike race.
Bear One sets the pace.

Count the bikes.
Count the wheels.
Which number is odd?
Which is even?

Bears Two and Four
crash and spill,
as they go speeding
down the hill.

Bears One, Three, and Five
are still in the race,
but Bear Number Five
can't keep the pace!

Bears One and Three
are still in the race.
It's even until . . .

That's not even!
That's odd!

MORE MATH FUN

- Count things in the world around you:
  - players in a game
  - parked cars
  - dishes on the table

  Is there an odd or an even number of each?

- Use coins or candies or buttons to prove the rules:
  - odd + odd = even
  - even + even = even
  - odd + even = odd

- What's your house number? Is it even or odd? What's the number on the house next door? What's the number on the house across the street? Where are the odd numbers? Where are the even numbers?

- Ask your mail carrier how he or she uses odd and even numbers.

one bear wins!

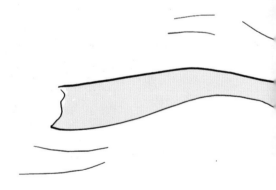